HANZEL AND PRETZEL

by Mike Thaler
Illustrated by Jared Lee

SCHOLASTIC INC.
New York Toronto London Auckland Sydney

For Brucie and Diana
—M.T.

To Beulah,
Mother. Friend. Angel.
—J.L.

ISBN 0-590-89827-2

Text copyright © 1997 by Mike Thaler.
Illustrations copyright © 1997 by Jared D. Lee Studio, Inc.
All rights reserved. Published by Scholastic Inc.
HAPPILY EVER LAUGHTER is a trademark of Mike Thaler and Jared Lee.
Library of Congress Catalog Card Number: 96-68252.

12 11 10 9 8 7 6 5 4 3 2 1   7 8 9/9 0 1 2/0

Printed in the U.S.A.   24

First Scholastic printing, March 1997

nce upon a time,
about 8:45,
there lived a brother and sister named Hanzel and Pretzel.
They lived with their parents near the Deep Dark Woods.
Every day their dad would warn them,
"Don't go into the Deep Dark Woods."
Every day Hanzel would ask, "Why not?"
And every day their mom would answer,
"Because you might get lost and meet the Horrible Witch,
who will eat you up."

But being a forgetful kid
with a lousy sense of direction,
Hanzel did lead Pretzel into the Woods, and they did get lost.
"I think we're lost," said Pretzel.
"No, we're not," said Hanzel.
He led Pretzel deeper into the Dark Woods.
"I think we're lost," said Pretzel.
"No, we're not," said Hanzel.
He led her still deeper into the Deep Dark Woods.

"I think we're lost," said Pretzel.
"I think you're right," said Hanzel,
and he began to cry.

"Look," said Pretzel,
"there's a cottage! I think it's the Witch's."
"No, it's not," said Hanzel, running up to the cottage,
which was made of gingerbread.

"I think it's the Witch's," said Pretzel.
"No, it's not," said Hanzel, biting into the doorknob.

Suddenly, the door opened,
and out stepped a witch with a nose like a pickle.

"I think it's the Witch," said Pretzel.
"I think you're right," said Hanzel, and he began to cry.

"Why are you eating my doorknob?" shrieked the Witch.

"Uh, trick or treat," said Pretzel.

"Is it Halloween already?" asked the Witch.

"Yes," said Pretzel.

"It was just Valentine's Day!" exclaimed the Witch.

"Time flies," said Pretzel.

"Well, then, come on in, kids,
and stay for dinner."

"Well, maybe just a snack," said Pretzel.

So Hanzel and Pretzel went inside.
They looked around.
Spiders crawled in each corner,
bats hung from every beam,
and a big cage sat in the middle of the floor.
"Who's your decorator?" asked Pretzel.
"Me," boasted the Witch.

"What's for dinner?" asked Hanzel.
"You!" shrieked the Witch.
"You don't want to eat him," pleaded Pretzel.
"He's very thin."
"Well," said the Witch, "we'll just fatten him up."
She shoved Hanzel into the cage.

Hanzel looked out through the bars and began to cry.
"Look on the bright side," joked Pretzel.
"At least we're not lost anymore."

The Witch put Pretzel to work polishing the kettle,
while every day she brought Hanzel a piece of her house to eat.

"Broom service!" she would cackle.
One day she fed him the door, the next day the porch.
Every day she felt his head to see if he was getting any fatter.

But Pretzel,
who was a quick thinker,
gave Hanzel a haircut every night.

"Eat, eat," clucked the Witch,
shoving a gingerbread chimney into the cage.
"Don't you have any cottage cheese?" asked Hanzel.

Weeks went by.
The pot was getting shinier,
and the Witch was getting hungrier.
Her stomach rumbled all night,
and she grumbled all day.

"You're eating me out of house and home, and you're not getting any fatter!"

"I'm going to cook you now!" shouted the Witch,
lighting the fire.
"Wok cooking is much healthier," said Hanzel.
"I'll give you a wok in the head," snorted the Witch.

Just then, Hanzel broke loose and ran around the pot.
The Witch chased him.
"You're fast food," she gasped.
"Bet you can't catch me," teased Hanzel.
"I don't play with my food," snarled the Witch.

As she leaned across the kettle to grab him,
Pretzel quickly pushed her in.
SPLASHO!

"What have you done?" wailed the Witch.
"Don't get yourself into a stew," piped Pretzel.
"We're having a slight change in the menu — it's pot luck!"

"We can make sand-witches," joked Hanzel.
"Or tea with an old bag."
"What about witches' stew?" suggested Pretzel.
"Witches' stew, what?" asked Hanzel.
"Witches' stew not scare me!" chuckled Pretzel.

Hanzel and Pretzel finished eating the cottage,
hopped on the broom, and flew home.

"Where've you been?" cried their mom.

"We just went to the corner to buy a broom," said Pretzel.

"It's been two weeks," said their dad. "You didn't go into the Deep Dark Woods, did you?"

"Not us," said Pretzel, crossing her fingers.

"We didn't meet the Horrible Witch, either," said Hanzel, crossing his eyes.

"You're lucky," said their dad. "She's supposed to be a really tough cookie."

Pretzel smiled.

"Oh, I don't know, Dad," she said.

"I hear she's not such a bad egg."

P.S. The Witch stopped being hard-boiled, became a vegetarian, and opened a health food store.